D1312616

A LETTER FROM SAINT NICHOLAS

To Children of Every Age

Christmas Blessings to you!

Fay Hornbecker

To Children of Every Age

A LETTER FROM
SAINT
NICHOLAS

BY JAY HORNBACHER
ILLUSTRATIONS BY MARGARITA SIKORSKAIA

A Letter from Saint Nicholas, To Children of Every Age © copyright 2019 by Jay Hornbacher. All rights reserved. No part of this book may be reproduced in any form whatsoever, by photography or xerography or by any other means, by broadcast or transmission, by translation into any kind of language, nor by recording electronically or otherwise, without permission in writing from the author, except by a reviewer, who may quote brief passages in critical articles or reviews.

This is a work of fiction. Names, characters, places, and incidents are either the products of the author's imagination or are used in a fictitious manner, and any resemblance to actual persons, living or dead, businesses, events, or locales is purely coincidental.

Selections from "In the Bleak Midwinter" reprinted from Christina Rossetti, *The Poetical Works of Christina Georgina Rossetti*, Macmillan (London, 1904).

Illustrated by Margarita Sikorskaia

ISBN 13: 978-1-64343-946-4
Library of Congress Catalog Number: 2019906407

Printed in the United States of America

First Printing: 2019
23 22 21 20 19   5 4 3 2 1

Book design and typesetting by Dan Pitts.

Beaver's Pond Press
7108 Ohms Lane
Edina, MN 55439–2129
(952) 829-8818
www.BeaversPondPress.com

To order, visit www.ItascaBooks.com or call (800) 901-3480 ext. 118.
Reseller discounts available.

Contact Jay Hornbacher at www.jayhornbacher.com for speaking engagements, book club discussions, and interviews.

To my daughter, Marya Hornbacher, who knows words.
To my wife, Gayle Bintliff, who knows hearts.
To my friend, Jay White, who knows me.

My dear children,

And there was light, YES! A dazzling burst of light when the world was spoken into being! The light is with us still, even in our deepest darkness, even in this darkening time of year.

You must come with me now, for I shall take you on a wondrous journey, I and a magical friend, where we will show you . . . Ah! But we shall reveal that mystery as we tell our story!

You know me by many names, but you may call me Nicholas. Perhaps you think me ancient, for I was born many centuries ago, and I lived to be an old man with long white hair and a beard like winter frost. It is said that in my long life I worked wonders and miracles, and that I was and am the giver of gifts at Christmastime. For these reasons, I am now called Saint Nicholas, but for you who enter this story, Nicholas will do. And I was young once, oh yes, full of life and love and laughter and mischief! Our family was wealthy beyond measure and gave lavishly and joyfully to those in need. Our lives seemed perfect.

Alas, my world turned dark when my parents died during a plague that took many lives, leaving me alone and adrift when I was only twenty years old. Their wealth became mine, but without them, it gave me neither comfort nor joy. My needs were simple, so I began to give gifts (secretly!) as my parents had done. This seemed to lift my spirits, and I gave away most of my possessions.

But I still felt empty and alone. Something was missing, something I could not name.

One winter night I had an enchanting dream in which I was wrapped in a powerful wind and carried over the earth and seas. As I hurtled through the air, I tried to see where the wind was taking me, but I could not tell. When I awoke, I knew at once the dream was telling me I must go on a journey in search of that place I had dreamed, where I might find healing and strength. Immediately I prepared to go, even in the bitter cold of December. I packed very little in my satchel, just a bit of food, and one gold coin. And I brought my open heart in hope that something would fill it.

My dream had told me to travel over mountains, so I would need a sure-footed donkey to carry me when the path became dangerous. A man in our village had several animals, so I walked to his house and knocked at the door. A large, burly man answered. He looked fierce, so I chose my words carefully.

"Sir," I said, "may I use one of your donkeys for a journey?"

He eyed me suspiciously. "Got money to pay?" he asked.

"Only this," I said, offering the one gold coin I had brought.

He stared at it with great disdain. "Can't let you use a donkey for that pittance," he said, turning to go.

"But, Father," piped a small voice from behind the door, "why can't he use Sebastian?"

"Hush, you whelp," said the man. "Sebastian's not going anywhere."

"But he's my donkey! You gave him to me," said the boy, "and I want the man to use him!"

I was eager to begin my journey, so I made bold to step into the doorway, where I saw a boy of about ten tugging at his father's cloak. "And who is Sebastian?" I said to the boy.

"He's my donkey," he said, and then he burst forth with a flood of words. "His name is Sebastian Jerome Wildears and he is a wonderful donkey and I love him and would gladly let you take him on your journey if only my father would let me!"

I turned to the man and said, "Sir, I truly am in need and will give the boy this gold coin for the use of . . . What was the donkey's name?"

"Sebastian Jerome Wildears," said the boy solemnly, looking at his father with pleading eyes.

Grumbling quietly, the man led us out to a small barn. It was so cold our breath came in great clouds, but inside, the barn was warm and the air was rich with the heavy scent of animals. We walked to a stall in a corner, where a small donkey with enormous ears lay staring into the distance, as if he could see something beyond our vision. He took no notice of us.

"This is Sebastian," said the boy proudly.

"He's not much of a beast," said the man, "but he may get you where you're going. One thing you need to know: you guide him by moving his ears. To go forward, move his ears forward; to the left or right, move them left or right; to speed up, tap on the back of his ears; to slow down, tap on the front of his ears. Got it?"

"What about stopping?" I asked.

"Squeeze his ears. Hard," said the man.

"But not too hard," the boy chimed in, getting the animal to his feet. He hugged Sebastian around the neck, and the donkey responded with a tender nuzzle.

"What shall I feed him?" I asked the boy, who replied, "Don't worry, he always finds food."

We started off, but the man growled, "Hey! Let's not forget to pay!" I gave my coin to the boy, who took it eagerly, as if he were being given rare treasure.

I waved good-bye and nudged Sebastian's ears forward. To my surprise, he ambled out of the stable and onto the road, and I walked alongside. As we departed, I heard the boy shout, "Good-bye, Sebastian. Be well on your journey."

And so we were off, this odd beast and I, in search of a place where my heart could be made whole. As we went along, I tested Sebastian's ears now and again and it was just as the man had said: ears to the left, turn left; ears to the right, turn right; and so on.

We traveled all morning, climbing higher and higher on the mountain trail until we reached a ridge well above where trees grew. I climbed onto Sebastian's back when walking became dangerous, and he stepped slowly on the rocky path, careful to avoid icy patches. In the early afternoon we stopped to rest and eat. I took an apple from my satchel and offered it to Sebastian, who sniffed at it, then turned and walked away to some low bushes. I ate the apple and was about to resume our journey, when Sebastian suddenly appeared, carrying in his mouth a branch laden with four oranges!

"Sebastian!" I exclaimed in amazement, "how did you . . . I mean, where did you . . . ?" But he dropped the branch, lay down next to me, and began munching on an orange. I watched him eat one orange, then another, and then a third, as I wondered how and where he had found oranges on a mountaintop in the dead of winter.

I put the last orange in my satchel and got up to leave. Snow began to fall, so I patted Sebastian on the side and said, "Come on, old fellow, we need to continue before darkness falls." He got to his feet and waited for me to climb on his back. And then we started off.

We rode in silence for some time as the snow began to fall faster, gathering on Sebastian's mane and my cloak. The wind blew sad notes, and my spirits sank with the darkening sky. Without even thinking, I said, "Sebastian, I am so sad and lonely. Have you ever felt that way?" Then I thought, *How foolish I have become, confessing my loneliness to a donkey!* Of course, he made no reply, but his left ear began twitching so wildly that I feared he might lose his balance.

I stroked him gently to calm him, and soon his ear was still again. The sky became ever darker, and I knew we must soon

find shelter for the night, but something drew me on. As we traveled into the light of a dimming sky, music came swirling into me from the wind, and with the music came words:

In the bleak midwinter, frosty wind made moan,
Earth stood hard as iron, water like a stone;
Snow had fallen, snow on snow, snow on snow,
In the bleak midwinter, long ago.

When I stopped singing, I noticed that Sebastian wasn't moving and was sniffing the air. His left ear was twitching again. I said, "Move on, Sebastian; we can't stop in this barren place."

But he stood still as a statue. I pointed his ears forward and tapped on the back of each one, but to no avail. It was as if my song had stopped him in his tracks.

Suddenly he began to trot straight ahead. I tapped his ears, turned his ears, and squeezed his ears, but he only went faster. Then, children, he took a sharp left turn, careening down an embankment so steep I thought I would be thrown onto the rocky ground! I pulled on his ears with all my might, but he just kept tearing down the mountainside, faster and faster, until we saw firelight in a town below. As we neared the town he broke into a gallop, and when we got there, he headed straight for an inn where people were crowding out the door and making a howling racket.

"Sebastian!" I cried, "I have no money for an inn!" But he
tore around the corner of the inn in great haste and headed for
the stable out back. *Ah,* I thought, *he wants a warm barn on this
cold night.*

When we reached the stable, he stopped so suddenly that I
was tossed to the ground! He trotted through the stable door,
and, curious, I picked myself up off the frozen ground and
followed him. It was warm inside, crowded with shepherds
young and old, animals of all sorts, and three men in royal
robes. The wild-eared donkey nosed his way to the center of
the group and kneeled.

I worked my way through the crowd to see what had interested him so, and there, lying on a bed of straw, was a newborn child—a baby, in the manger, of all places! A young woman and an older man, both looking exhausted, sat next to the babe. I guessed they were the parents and was about to ask them why they would bring a child to such a place on a cold night, when I heard strange noises from Sebastian, a loud and urgent groaning. And then, children, he began braying as if he would sing, and made sounds that—no, this donkey made . . . *words!*

> *Our God, heaven cannot hold Him, nor earth sustain;*
> *Heaven and earth shall flee away, when He comes to reign.*
> *In the bleak midwinter a stable place sufficed*
> *The Lord God Almighty, Jesus Christ.*

The child's mother reached out and gently petted Sebastian's nose. He made soft sounds, and great round tears fell from his eyes. As each tear touched the ground, it became a beautiful red rose—roses, in the depth of winter! The young mother took one of the roses and put it next to the child in the manger.

Suddenly it struck me with great force—not only had seeing the child inspired my donkey companion to speech, not only had he uttered something like song, but he had sung that the child in the manger was the baby Jesus!

"But, Sebastian," I said, "this is not possible! We live more than three hundred years after Jesus was born. We cannot be … where we are!"

He nudged me in the ribs with his nose and said, "Hush, Nicholas. Let the miracle happen."

I was about to protest when I felt a rush of wind and heard whispering, as if something new and beautiful and utterly enchanting had found us. I felt a soft breeze on my cheeks and the eerie touch of wings. The light in the stable became ever brighter, and the sound stopped, giving way to a stillness filled with expectation. Then I heard a voice that was fresh and new, yet ancient and familiar:

> *Enough for Him, whom cherubim, worship night and day,*
> *Breastful of milk, and a mangerful of hay;*
> *Enough for Him, whom angels fall before,*
> *The ox and ass and camel which adore.*

The young mother, who was not much older than a girl herself,
bent down and kissed the child. He smiled and began feeding
at her breast. As he did, I heard the whispering again and felt
the breeze, warm and gentle. Then I knew there were angels
present, and that they, too, had sung praises.

I turned to Sebastian and said, "So this *is* the Holy Child!" Sebastian looked at me with moist eyes, smiling and nodding. Then all was still while everyone offered gifts.

The three old men in fine robes each gave a small chest in which there seemed to be rare treasures. The older shepherds gave lambs, and one shepherd boy placed a small shiny object near the child. Sebastian had given tears that were transformed into roses. The other animals placed fur and hide and feathers before the child in the manger. I noticed that everyone was glancing at me, as if they expected something. Finally, Sebastian put his soft mouth to my ear and said, "Nicholas, where is *your* gift?"

I felt ashamed, because I had nothing to offer. I whispered, "Sebastian, I gave away most of my possessions and traveled with almost nothing. I have no gift."

If donkeys can frown, I am sure Sebastian frowned at me. He said, "Nicholas, have you *nothing* to offer?" Finally I remembered I had one orange left in my satchel, so I offered it to the young mother and meekly sang this bit of song:

What can I give Him, poor as I am?
If I were a shepherd, I would bring a lamb;
If I were a wise man, I would do my part;
Yet what I can I give Him: give Him my heart.

When she placed the orange in the manger along with the other gifts, the baby awoke and looked straight at me. He smiled. My dear children, I have never seen such eyes! These small eyes wrapped me in a love deeper and richer than any I had ever known, a love that has been with me always and that I knew I must share with any and all. Finally, Jesus blinked softly, laid down his head, and slept.

We could hear sounds of revelry from the inn, but no noise could disturb the holy silence in which we were cradled, held in a tenderness beyond all hope and desire. Finally, not wanting the moment to end, we left the family, knowing the child's father would guard the mother and babe with his life. The shepherds departed to the hills. The animals went back to their stalls. Two of the old men had fallen asleep, and the third woke them and guided them to the inn. Sebastian and I found an empty stall and curled up together in the straw. We lay awake for a long time, bathed in light from a great star.

When I was almost asleep, I heard Sebastian say, "Nicholas, do you know what it means, that you gave your heart to the child?"

"Not quite," I said, "but I think I may know someday."

"Oh, yes," said Sebastian. "You will."

Then we slept. And I dreamed once again, this time of empty shoes and sad hearts and lonely lives. As time passed and I grew in years and wisdom, I knew my dream had told me I must fill shoes with small treasures, hearts with leaping hope, and lives with tender love.

I awoke to a bitterly cold morning and moved to get closer to Sebastian. But he was gone! I sprang to my feet and looked everywhere for him—in the stable, in the barnyard, everywhere! I asked at the inn if anyone had seen a small donkey with very long ears. A man replied, "I saw him leave early this morning. He carried a woman and a child on his back, and a man walked next to them. Someone said they were traveling to Egypt. Imagine that! Egypt!"

At once, I knew that, yes! I had seen the holy family, now traveling to Egypt for their own safety. I was not lost in a dream but found and restored, with a healed heart. I did not understand the mystery of that wondrous night, but as Sebastian had urged me to do, I let the miracle happen.

Suddenly it dawned on me that not only had I traveled far from my village, but I had gone back in time three hundred years! Looking around, I saw that I was still near the inn and the stable, and that nothing about the surroundings had changed, despite the wonder of the night. I looked at the nearby hills and saw shepherds tending their flocks. There was no doubt I was still in Bethlehem.

I didn't know what to do or where to go, so I began walking toward the edge of the little town, onto an open road. After I had walked for a while, I looked back—and children, the town was gone! I saw only a light blue mist where it had stood!

I stared for some time, thinking it would appear again, but I saw nothing through the mist. Then I realized the mist was all around me, as if I were standing in clouds! I took hesitant steps, uncertain where the road would lead. As I walked, the mist began to clear. Soon a house came into view, and then another and another and another. As I came closer, I saw that I was walking toward my own village, and in the distance, I saw my own house! I was home!

But my excitement vanished when I remembered that I would have to explain Sebastian's disappearance. I walked to the house where I had found this magical donkey and saw the man and his son working in the barnyard. I approached them hesitantly.

"Sir," I said to the man, "I'm afraid I've lost your donkey."

He stared at me as though I had lost my mind. "What donkey are you talking about?"

"Sebastian," I said. "The donkey you let me use yesterday."

"Never heard of him," said the man. "You must have the wrong house. Either that or you're crazy. Come on, boy," he said. "Let's get away from this madman."

I looked after them, sputtering in amazement as they walked away. But as they entered their house, the boy—whom I knew I had seen in the night—looked back at me, winked, and then vanished! I stared in astonishment, then realized that he, too, had traveled through time and space, captured by wonder and love. I walked to my own home, knowing all was well, and knowing that I had not found Sebastian; he had found me, long ago, so very long ago.

My beloved children, as you sleep and dream this night, remember Sebastian, who taught me about oranges and roses and mystery. Know that the gift of Jesus' birth is yours in every season, and that the light shines and shines and ever shines in the darkness. God bless you all, young and old! I shall cherish forever the miracle of every one of you.

With love from my heart to yours,

Saint Nicholas